Future World

Spaceship Earth

The architectural icon for Epcot is a geodesic sphere, which contains a ride-through adventure highlighting milestones in communication from the earliest prehistoric cave paintings to the satellite technologies of today and the possibilities for the future. Spaceship Earth is based on the concept developed by science-fiction writer Ray Bradbury that Earth is man's vehicle in space.

Spaceship Earth by the Numbers	
2	spheres—one is inside the other
2 years, 2 months	construction time (40,800 labor hours)
3	pairs of legs
16	million pounds of weight
165	feet in diameter
180	height in feet—18 stories above ground level
518.1	feet in circumference
1,700	tons of steel
11,324	aluminum and plastic-alloy individual triangles on the exterior
40,000	years of human history compressed in the ride-through
150,000	square feet of exterior surface area
500,000	weight in pounds of entire steel structure
2,200,000	cubic feet of volume

Universe of Energy

Universe of Energy is an exploration of the forces that fuel our lives and the universe itself. In the opening movie, Ellen is watching a game show on TV, in which her college roommate, Judy Peterson, is competing. As she tries to play along at home, Ellen quickly realizes her ignorance on the topic of energy. But fortunately, her neighbor Bill Nye (the Science Guy!) comes by and gives her a crash course in "Energy 101." Viewers then accompany Ellen on an odyssey through a primeval world full of huge prehistoric trees, unearthly fogs, volcanoes, and battling dinosaurs. At the conclusion, Ellen dreams of playing against Judy on the game show, betting everything in the final round, when she must name the one energy source that will never be depleted. (She gets it right—it's brain power.)

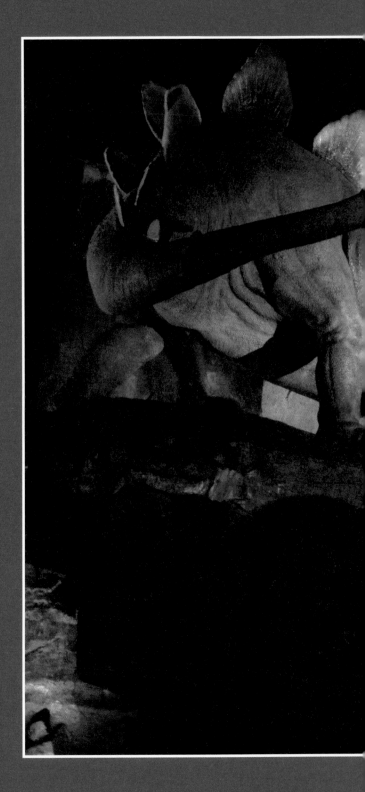

FACTOIDS

- Two acres of the roof are covered with 80,000 photovoltaic cells that can produce up to 70,000 watts of direct current power, enough to supply the needs of 15 single-family homes.

- For a primeval diorama, 3 artists spent 5,700 hours painting a backdrop 32 feet high and 515 feet long.

- The history of the universe is shown in only 60 seconds.

- Six 97-passenger vehicles weighing 30,000 pounds each are guided along on a $\frac{1}{8}$-inch thick wire embedded in the concrete floor.

- The 3 dinosaur topiaries outside the pavilion represent the stegosaurus, the tyrannosaurus, and the sauropod.

Mission: SPACE

Would-be astronauts rocket from a liftoff sequence through a slingshot maneuver around the moon to an asteroid-dodging pinpoint landing on Mars as they utilize NASA training techniques in Mission: SPACE. In the Recruiting Center, cadets are separated into one of two teams for different intensities of training. Following a briefing session in the International Space Training Center (ISTC), travelers are assigned their roles (pilot, navigator, engineer, or commander), then sit side by side in space capsules. Orange Team members will also experience G-forces and a momentary sensation of weightlessness as they and the Green Team complete unique mission tasks while experiencing the thrills and challenges of space flight.

Mission: SPACE by the Numbers	
1	minute—time it takes for the Gravity Wheel in the Space Simulation Lab to rotate
2	primary computers on the ride system that control the ride
16	diameter in feet of Jupiter in Planetary Plaza
25	space experts from NASA and the Jet Propulsion Lab who worked with Walt Disney Imagineers to create the story and design of the attraction
29	missions between 1959 and 1976 that the United States and Russia sent to the moon that are noted on the moon sphere in Planetary Plaza
32	diameter in feet of Gravity Wheel
35	height in feet of Gravity Wheel
100	shades of red considered for the color of the red planet on the pavilion's facade

MISSION: FACTS

↵ It would take 13,136,640 jellybeans to fill the Earth sphere in Planetary Plaza. 53, 809, 920 would fill the Jupiter sphere and 22,702,080 would fill the moon.

↵ The Lunar Rover vehicle in the pre-show area, on loan from the Smithsonian Institute, is one of only four vehicles of its kind.

Test Track

Buckle up and brace yourself for the longest, fastest ride in Walt Disney World! Test Track allows riders to get an insider's view of the exclusive world of automobile testing. It's one of the most complex attractions at Epcot—the computers inside each vehicle have more processing power than the computers aboard a space shuttle.

Test Track by the Numbers	
1	length in miles (more or less) of the course
2	million—number of miles the vehicles travel in one year
3	computers inside each vehicle
4,500	number of times the car crashes in the Barrier test (Yes, it really crashes, then resets.)

PERFORMANCE TESTS

- **Hill Climb:** Race up an 18-degree-angle, 3-story hill with everything your car's got. But remember—what goes up must come down!

- **Suspension:** Some roads are less than ideal, and you better hope your shocks are working. Road surfaces include the wicked Belgian Block!

- **Brakes:** Leave every cone standing. Yeah, right!

- **Environmental Chamber:** If you can't take the heat—that's okay. Next comes a 100-degree shift from arid desert to arctic cold.

- **Ride Handling:** You never know what's down the road, and this test is proof. There's a highway's worth of surprises in your headlights as you drive through a mean mountain switchback.

- **Barrier:** In real vehicle test facilities, crash-test dummies are used to measure the impact of high-speed, head-on collisions. Here, the pleasure is all yours.

- **High Speed:** Negotiate some outrageously sharp, banked curves (including one at a 50-degree angle), testing your car's ability to hug the roads at a high speed—up to 65 miles per hour. *Wheeeeeeeeeeeeeeeeeeeee!*

The Seas with Nemo and Friends

Board a clamobile and follow Marlin and Dory from Disney•Pixar's *Finding Nemo* as they search for the little clown fish, who has once again taken off on his own. Voyagers pass through the Coral Caves beach area, where the surf level is *Just Swell*, then slip under pier pilings that lead them underwater and into a new adventure with all their oceanic friends, which include the sea anemones that are Nemo's home, and a jellyfish forest, and the EAC (East Australian Current), where Nemo and his totally tubular terrapin buddy, Squirt, ride the underwater waves. Along the way, there's a little danger, a lot of laughs, and an incredible finale, when your clamobile enters the gigantic aquarium where Nemo and all his friends actually appear to swim alongside the real-life creatures of the coral reef.

After the ride's over, you're encouraged to "come out of your shell," and visit the Seas pavilion, which represents the world's largest man-made ocean environment—containing 5.7 million gallons of water. Here, you can view endangered manatees, chameleonlike cuttlefish, dolphins, and colorful parrot fish, among the more than 3,000 species of marine life, which live in environments ranging from a Pacific Coast kelp forest to a simulated Caribbean coral-reef setting.

Bruce's Sub House

In an interactive play area inside the pavilion, young fish fans can learn about sharks and grab a photo op with the leader of the "Fish are Friends, not Food" movement.

Mr. Ray's Pop Quiz

You don't have to join a school of fish like Nemo to take this informative test. After completing it, you can be e-mailed a certificate for passing the course. What grade do you get? Why, a Sea-Plus, of course!

Turtle Talk with Crush

"That's a really cool color shell you're wearing, dude!" Here's where you can gab with Crush, the 150-year-old sea turtle who's always ready for a little conversation on the hydrophone as he talks to his friends in the "human tank." Righteous!

Living with The Land

Voyagers set sail on a boat ride journeying through a tropical rain forest, the African desert, the American plains, and the farms of yesteryear, all showcasing the research and work of The Land science team. In these greenhouses of the future, the latest developments in aquaculture and desert farming are revealed, as well as imaginative ways to grow crops—hanging them in the air or growing them without soil are two possibilities. Each year more than 30 tons of fruits and vegetables grown in The Land pavilion and 6,500 pounds of bass, catfish, and tilapia from the aquaculture area are served in Walt Disney World restaurants.

Circle of Life

Simba, Pumbaa, and Timon from Walt Disney's *The Lion King* roar to life in a lighthearted showpiece about the environment, combining animation and live action in a filmed fable. It seems Timon and Pumbaa want to open the Hakuna Matata Lakeside Village, a decidedly non-ecological resort, so Simba must show them how important the different kinds of plants and animals are to the health of the planet. After all, they're part of the Circle of Life!

PARTIAL LIST OF CROPS

Mickey Mouse–shaped cucumbers

Mickey Mouse–shaped watermelons

"Cinderella" pumpkins

Nine-pound lemons (the size of bowling balls)

Guinness World Record–holding tomato tree

Soarin'

A bird's-eye view of California is provided by a breathtaking glide over the majestic natural wonders of the Golden State. Soarin' literally lifts passengers forty feet aloft into a giant, projection-screen dome using breakthrough motion-based technology. This exciting, wind-in-your-hair adventure ride takes you over towering redwoods and waterfalls, snow-capped mountains, expansive deserts, and the crashing waves of the Pacific coast, providing an extraordinary sensation of free flight. You may be tempted to pull your feet up to avoid banging them on the Golden Gate Bridge! The sensations of this exhilarating aerial journey are intensified with the fragrances of orange blossoms and pine trees.

The Tile Mosaics

The two 134-foot-long tile mosaics at the entrance cover 3,000 square feet. There are 150,000 individually cut and shaped pieces of marble, granite, slate, smalto, Venetian glass, 14-karat gold, mirror, ceramic, and pebble pieces, in 131 colors, representing the layers of the earth. The artist added one small thing to keep the mosaics from being mirror images—a small green tile on the right side's mural that's a little tribute to his family.

Journey Into Imagination with Figment

It's open house at the Imagination Institute, and Dr. Nigel Channing (Chairman, Principal Scientist, Director of Operations, Head of Laboratories, and Manager of Everything Else) is happy to welcome the public in to visit the Sensory Labs, where he will show visitors how to capture and control their imagination through the senses. Boarding trams invented by Dr. Wayne Szalinski, participants begin their ride through the laboratories. But Channing's own creation, the free-spirited purple dragon Figment (for which he won Inventor of the Year), is determined to show us the most important aspect of one's imagination—it works best when it's free!

THE POSSIBILITIES ARE ENDLESS

THE FIRST RULE OF IMAGINATION: THERE ARE NO RULES

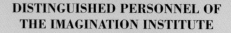

DISTINGUISHED PERSONNEL OF THE IMAGINATION INSTITUTE

Dr. Phillip Brainard,
Inventor of Flubber

Dr. Wayne Szalinski,
Inventor of the Shrinking Machine

Dexter Reilly
(who left his tennis shoes in the computer lab)

Wilby Daniels
(always ready to tell a shaggy-dog story)

Merlin Jones
(whose monkeys are loose again!)

IF YOU CAN IMAGINE IT, YOU CAN DO IT

Honey, I Shrunk the Audience

This is the year that Dr. Wayne Szalinski is finally being honored as Inventor of the Year by the Imagination Institute. Chairman Dr. Nigel Channing is on hand to present the award, but things go awry (as usual) when the shrinking machine accidentally shrinks the audience! This amazing 3-D film features a dog with an itchy nose, an unhappy snake, and—watch out for those mice!

World Showcase

Where else can you travel from Mexico to Canada (passing nine other countries in between) in only 1.2 miles? A trip around the world is a daily experience for visitors of the World Showcase at Epcot. Exotic cuisine, entertainment, artisans, cultural ambassadors dressed in traditional costumes, and scenic wonders abound. The journey begins around a forty-acre lagoon where the World Showcase pavilions dot the shores with re-creations of architectural landmarks and historic scenes familiar to world travelers. Built with finite attention to detail, the buildings, streets, gardens, and monuments give an authentic visual experience of each land, entertaining and informing visitors as well as providing a two-way cultural exchange for the young men and women from each country who work in the showcases. Adding to the global celebration is the fireworks spectacular performed nightly, IllumiNations: Reflections of Earth.

Mexico

A lively marketplace and authentic mariachi bands characterize the *caliente* flavor of this ancient culture. After passing through a "jungle" landscape of lush hibiscus, palm trees, and cacti, explorers come upon a temple ruin. The architecture and design of the impressive pyramid is a fusion of third-century Mesoamerican components, fronted by a carved tableau of the god Quetzalcóatl.

The interior blends features from several epochs of the country's pre-Columbian civilizations—Mayan, Toltec, and Aztec—as well as the legacy of its Spanish affiliation. The gallery inside represents a Mayan ceremonial hall complete with temple columns.

Visitors pass under an Aztec calendar on their way to the Plaza de los Amigos—Plaza of Friends—where they enter a formal portico, modeled after a mayor's mansion. It's set in eternal nighttime, lit by lanterns and the glow of a smoking volcano in the distance.

Gran Fiesta Tour Starring The Three Caballeros

The Three Caballeros—Donald Duck, Jose Carioca, and Panchito—from the 1944 film are back together again in a new multimedia attraction. In Mexico City for a grand performance, Donald disappears to take in the sights of the city, so Jose and Panchito go in search of their missing friend.

Norway

The first thing you see in the Norway pavilion is a Stavekirke, or Stave Church—a striking wooden structure styled after Gol Church of Hallingdal, built around 1250 AD. Stave churches date back as early as 1015 and were common in every village; the few remaining structures in the country are now nationally protected. Adorned with tiers of dragon heads, this Stavekirke houses exhibits of Norse artifacts.

The pavilion's maritime setting exemplifies the rich history of this sea-faring society. The cobblestoned town plaza evokes the coastal cities of Bergen, Alesund, and Oslo, and the backdrop for the showcase is a castle styled after Akershus, a fourteenth-century fortress that overlooks the heart of Oslo's harbor.

All the exteriors reflect the finishes and materials used in Norwegian architecture and ornamentation. The roof over the Kringla Bakeri og Kafe's seating area is covered in real sod!

Maelstrom

Travelers embark on a voyage that takes a look at Norwegian mythology and folklore in Maelstrom. After the Norse god Odin invites you to join the adventure, riders sail from a tenth-century Viking village on a dragon-headed longboat patterned on the actual crafts used by the Vikings. This excursion through time features treacherous rapids, waterfalls, and a very tricky three-headed troll. Passengers must hold on tight as they plummet *backward* past polar bears and ice floes into the stormy North Sea! A five-minute post-ride film focuses on modern Norway and its industries.

China

The gateway to the China pavilion is based on the main gate at the emperor's summer palace in Beijing—the Zhao Yang Men, or Gate of the Golden Sun. The Hall of Prayer for Good Harvest embodies the agricultural theme carried throughout the pavilion. Inside, four columns represent the seasons of the year and twelve shorter columns represent both the months and the twelve-year cycle the Chinese live by. The red and yellow colors represent, respectively, happiness and the power of the emperor. Circles indicating heaven and squares signifying earth are frequent motifs in the design.

The public marketplace, designed to encourage so- cializing, includes facades borrowed from an elegant home, a schoolhouse, a city gate, and shop fronts reflect- ing European overtones. Set on the Xing Fu Jie, or Street of Good Fortune, the market- place exemplifies the narrow city streets of this densely populated country. Within the pavilion, gardens and a reflecting pond symbol- izing the order and discipline of nature, simulate those found in Suzhou.

The one-half-scale reproduction of the Forbidden City's Temple of Heaven, through which guests pass into a Circle-Vision 360 theater, symbolizes the Chinese universe. *Reflections of China* takes viewers to exotic sites, such as Beijing's Forbidden City, Mongolia, and Shanghai. The original film was replaced in 2003 to better showcase the changes that have occurred in the nation of China over the past twenty years, though it is still hosted by Li Bai, the immortal poet from the eighth- century Tang Dynasty.

Germany

The German pavilion transports visitors to authentic surroundings inspired by towns along the Rhine and in Bavaria. The high castle walls that serve as a backdrop are a combination of elements from Eltz Castle near Koblenz on the Mosel River and Stahleck Fortress on the Rhine.

The facade of the Das Kaufhaus is based on a sixteenth-century merchants' hall located in the Black Forest with the same name but with one significant difference. On the original structure, four statues recall the reign of the Hapsburg emperors (1273–1918), but the scale of the pavilion necessitated that one be left off. Maximilian I was unable to join the other rulers—only Philip I, Charles V, and Ferdinand I stand guard.

The Platz (Plaza) includes a glockenspiel, which rings out a musical composition unique to the pavilion, and a sculpture, modeled after the statue in Rothenburg of St. George and the Dragon. St. George is a symbol of protection, a common site in town squares. Other facades in the village are inspired by sources such as buildings in Freiburg and the four-hundred-year-old Römerberg Plaz in Frankfurt. The Biergarten Restaurant is derived from a biergarten in the 500-year-old town of Rothenberg ob der Tauber, and is decorated with ornate medieval crests.

The Romantic Road train and miniature countryside that are to the right of the pavilion portray life in a typical German village between Füssen and Würzburg. The installation's landscape changes with the seasons.

Italy

The romance and beauty of Italy are featured in a pastiche of elegant architectural styles and ornamental decorations, primarily represented by a reproduction of the Doge's Palace and a one-fifth, scaled-down version of the Campanile (bell tower) on the Piazza di San Marco—St. Mark's Square—in Venice. Sculptures on towering columns mirror those

on the original piazza, portraying the Lion of St. Mark, protector of the city of Venice (on the left), and St. Theodore and the Dragon (to the right). Complementing all this are Venetian bridges and gondolas moored to colorful barber poles.

The paving around the Campanile is patterned after that of St. Mark's Square, and the bell tower sports an angel covered in gold leaf, just like the original. Unlike the original, the square has been flipped—in order to ensure a better balance of structures in World Showcase. Other buildings are reminiscent of the Florentine style, while Arcata d'Artigiani, with its stucco edifice and claylike roofing, brings together components from rural regions around Tuscany.

The garden wall enclosing the piazza is similar to many in Rome and Florence. Throughout the pavilion are olive, kumquat, and cypress trees—staples of the Italian landscape. The fountain here, like the ones prevalent in other Italian cities, is a heroic version of the Fontana di Nettuno, or Neptune Fountain. It was inspired by the fountains sculpted by Gian Lorenzo Bernini and Trevi Fountain in Rome (of "three coins" popularity).

Japan

Architecture and landscaping meld exquisitely in the Japan pavilion. The blue-roofed Goju No To Pagoda is a five-story structure, modeled after the eighth-century Horyuji Temple in Nara. Each story represents one of the elements—the first level is earth, then water, fire, wind, and finally sky, signifying heaven. Topping the pagoda is a nine-ringed bronze spire, known as a "sorin," that sports gold wind chimes and an abstract water flame.

The structure that houses the Mitsukoshi Department Store on the first floor and a formal Japanese restaurant on the second was inspired by a portion of the Gosho Imperial Palace in Kyoto, known as the Shishinden, or Great Hall of Ceremonies. Our modern-day department stores can trace their roots back to Japan during the Tokugawa Shogun era.

The Yakitori House is a replica of the Katsura Imperial Villa in Kyoto. Built in the sixteenth century, it blends royal culture with the simple yet refined style of early Japanese architecture in a perfectly balanced building. In a serene area outside, rocks, symbolizing the long life of the earth, combine with water, symbolizing the sea, which the Japanese consider a source of life.

The Torii Gate at the Lagoon edge is modeled after one that stands at the Itsukushima Shrine on the Inland Sea. Toriis were originally conceived as perches where roosters would welcome the sun goddesses, and they gradually developed into large gates. Resembling a giant calligraphic character, the Gate of Honor is a popular good luck symbol.

The American Adventure by the Numbers	
2	feathers worn by Chief Joseph, symbolizing peace
4	different shades of white that were used in painting the building from top to bottom
8	identical chandeliers
10	height in feet of the dome in the Rotunda
12	columns in The American Adventure Rotunda
18	cents per gallon of gas during the Depression scene
24	computers that control the operation of the show
35	total height in feet of the Rotunda
35	Audio-Animatronics characters on stage
155	length in feet of screen (height is 28 feet—the longest rear-projection screen in existence)
175	weight in tons of the 65-foot by 45-foot hydraulic scene changer that moves the show sets into place
180	weight in pounds of each chandelier
319	audio speakers
350	years of our nation's history portrayed in this drama
1,024	seats in the theater
108,555	total footage in square feet
110,000	bricks in the facade

The American Adventure

The American Adventure is not a pavilion in the same sense as the others in World Showcase. Since it is primarily a show and not designed to represent the experience of visiting another country as are the other pavilions, the showcase and the show bear the same name. Since it represents the host nation, the creators and designers felt that the building should be centrally placed—and be visible from across the Lagoon.

The show, set in what is intended to be seen as the "people's mansion," is based on a variety of architectural influences. From the late 1790s to around 1830, American public architecture was made up of a mixture of styles, including English Georgian, which was developed during the reign of King George III and captured the spirit of the American Revolution. The American Adventure combines several classic Georgian-style buildings, including examples from Williamsburg, Virginia; Independence Hall in Philadelphia; the Old State House in Boston; and Thomas Jefferson's home, Monticello. Surrounding the pavilion is a landscape of flowers in red, white, and blue.

The American Adventure presents an inspirational story of the United States of America and its people in a multimedia mix of song, music, art, and Audio-Animatronics technology, showcasing important moments in American history. Host figures Mark Twain and Benjamin Franklin, who was the first Audio-Animatronics character to walk up a flight of stairs (to visit Thomas Jefferson), join with the audience to view the conflicts and successes that strengthened the American character and to affirm that the greatest resource the United States has is its people.

On your way to the second floor, note the awe-inspiring Hall of Flags, which serves as a colorful reminder of the many flags that have flown over the United States during the course of American history.

Morocco

The Koutoubia Minaret, a detailed replica of a famous prayer tower in Marrakesh, stands guard over the entrance to the Morocco pavilion, where the Moroccan cities of Casablanca, Fez, and Marrakesh are represented. Morocco is the only pavilion in World Showcase that is sponsored by its nation's government. The King of Morocco wanted to insure its authenticity so he sent over a large contingent of native artisans, including nineteen Moroccan *maalems*, to work on the intricate architectural details of the structures. They spent months re-creating the colorful tile masterpieces of this North African country.

Like most Moroccan cities, the pavilion is divided into two sections: the Ville Nouvelle (new city) in front and the Medina (old city) in back. The entrance to the Medina is through the pointed arches and swirling blue designs of Bab Boujouloud Gate, a replica of a gateway in the city of Fez. Just inside is Fez House, a re-creation of a traditional Moroccan home. Also in the Medina is a reproduction of the Chella Minaret, from the capital city of Rabat, which rises above the souks (shops) and shoppers in the thriving marketplace.

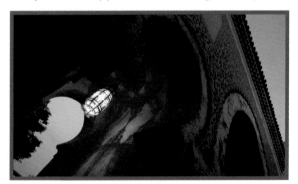

A reproduction of the Nejjarine Fountain in Fez el Bali represents the traditional village fountain in the center of a rectangular courtyard. Its ornate edifice is lined with thousands of multicolored tiles, whose design aesthetic consists of intricate, abstract geometric patterns. Nine tons of handmade, hand-cut tiles were used in the authentic mosaics throughout the pavilion.

France

The France pavilion reflects the ambience of the time between 1870 and 1910, a period known as La Belle Epoque, or the "beautiful age," an energetic era of art and literature, inventions and science, when a diversity of styles formed the character of Paris boulevards and architecture. Within the showcase

are the Beaux Arts Librarie et Galerie, reflective of the Art Nouveau style; and Plume et Palette, a perfume shop patterned after the chateau look of an older Paris. Sidewalk tables and fountains abound near the Chefs de France restaurant, a scaled-down version of a nineteenth-century building, featuring green patina-colored mansard roofs and elegant ironwork. Le Petit Rue, a provincial street, reflects a village atmosphere. The Eiffel Tower here is approximately one-tenth the height of the actual tower in Paris and was constructed using Gustave Eiffel's original blueprints.

The stunning two-hundred-degree panoramic film *Impressions de France* is shown in the Palais du Cinema, which was inspired by the palatial Chateau de Fontainebleau outside Paris. Its facade is a classical portico; and the interior is modeled after Les Halles, the busy garden market of Paris. In this travelogue set to classical music, viewers race cars in Cannes, ride boats on the Seine, ski over dangerously rocky peaks, take a train ride into Paris, and even climb the Eiffel Tower itself.

The bridge that connects the France pavilion and the United Kingdom pavilion is a replica of the Pont des Arts, a pedestrian bridge that crosses the Seine. Beside the river, a young painter has parked his bicycle. Perhaps he is taking a nap after visiting La Maison du Vins?

United Kingdom

Time, material, and style are all compressed into a single combination of city, town, and rural atmosphere in the United Kingdom pavilion. The building styles advance chrono*logically* in a clockwise circle from thatched-roofed cottages of the 1500s (the time of William Shakespeare) in The Tea Caddy, to the Victorian era (1800s) of the Rose and Crown Pub.

An exquisite hedge maze flows out onto Lower Regency Street, which itself flows into a typical Hyde Park bandstand. Coming around Upper Regency Street onto Tudor Lane, past The Toy Soldier shop (where a package waits to be picked up by A.A. Milne, the author of the Winnie the Pooh stories), are a town gate and clock tower representative of York.

The motto of the Rose and Crown Pub on High Street is expressed on the sign in front—*Otium cum Dignitate*—which translates from the Latin as "leisure with dignity." Here, imbibers can enjoy the best British stout and ale (served not at the traditional English room temperature, but cold) around a horseshoe-shaped bar or at tall tables.

The Crown and Crest Historical Research Center, a brick, 1400s-style house, looks out onto a city square complete with a sundial-embellished "roundabout" column, copying a look found in London and Edinburgh. Beside it, The Sportsman's Shoppe sports an exterior facade similar to that of King Henry VIII's Hampton Court of the 1600s. Throughout the pavilion are several scarlet phone booths and lovely, flower-filled maze gardens.

Canada

In the Canada pavilion, every province is represented, and examples of buildings and scenes found throughout the nation are presented on several tiers. On the first level, a First Nation village introduces the culture of the Northwest. It features three carved totem poles, including one that tells the story of how Raven tricked the Chief of the Skies.

On the second level, a Nova Scotia sea village is set on the left, while Quebec City is on the right. A nineteenth-century French château-style hotel is replicated in the Hôtel du Canada. Opposite the hotel is a stone building modeled after a famous landmark near Niagara Falls. This building reflects the British influence in Canada, while a nearby waterfront area has the look of the eastern seaboard. On the far lower side of the pavilion, the lovely Victoria Gardens are based on the Butchart Gardens of British Columbia's west coast, whose credo is that horticulture is a work of art and a labor of love.

The backdrop to all this are the stunning Canadian Rockies, presented in a setting complete with steep mountains, thundering waterfalls, and a tall northern forest. The fir trees that sit atop the mountains are cultivated for three years, giving them time to adapt to the Florida climate before they are displayed. They're not actually planted among the rocks, but rather placed in between them in plastic tubs. *O' Canada*, housed underneath, is a Circle-Vision 360 film that allows viewers to participate in a dogsled race, watch a hockey game, and ride in the Calgary stampede rodeo.

Dining Around the World

The restaurants of World Showcase offer authentic cuisine from around the globe, served in picturesque settings that add to the international flavor of the menu.

In Mexico, the San Angel Inn offers tortillas served with beef, chicken, and cheese fillings. One highlight is chicken *mole poblano*, which combines chiles and cocoa, among other ingredients, for its unique, rich sauce.

The Akershus Royal Banquet Hall inside Norway has a varied menu that starts with a *koldtbord* (cold table) including meats and seafood, followed by the *smarvarmt*, or hot dishes, with samplings of venison, lamb, and *Kjottkake*, a mixture of beef and pork. Desserts feature a traditional and luscious rice cream topped with strawberries.

Oktoberfest is celebrated every day at the Biergarten restaurant in the Germany pavilion with a festive show featuring German songs and an oompah band that encourages patrons to sing and yodel along with its lederhosen-clad members. A sumptuous buffet features modern German cuisine served from skillets and Crock-Pots, giving the meal a home-cooked feel. The chef offers seasonal vegetables such as snow peas and green beans, and fresh salmon and trout prepared with light, flavorful sauces. At the Sommerfest next door, tasty bratwurst and pretzels are available.

In China, dragons are considered powerful, protective creatures. The number nine is also powerful and lucky. These two forces are brought together as diners enjoy tasty epicurean adventures from five Chinese provinces at Nine Dragons Restaurant. In addition to the familiar *Moo Gu Gai Pan* and sweet and sour pork, the Nine Dragons menu offers everything from sirloin steak to Cantonese-style prepared lobster. Appetizers include pot stickers, spring rolls, and Drunken Chicken. Kiangche-style entrees include stir-fried scallops and vegetables. Szechuan/Hunan-style dishes feature chicken, shrimp, and lobster, brought to life with hot peppers and spicy sauces. Enjoy Singapore Rice Vermicelli, Xinjiang lamb chops, or Kiangche honey-sesame chicken, all eaten under the watchful eyes of dragon-decorated ceiling tiles.

Japan offers many dining options in diverse settings. Overlooking tranquil gardens, Yakitori House features its namesake broiled skewers of chicken basted with teriyaki sauce, as well as uniquely Japanese desserts such as green tea or ginger ice cream. In the Mitsukoshi complex, the Matsunoma Lounge serves sushi and tempura, while in Teppanyaki's five teppan rooms, chefs prepare the entrees on grills set into the dining tables.

Restaurant Marrakesh in Morocco serves flavorful North African delicacies, including couscous with chicken, lamb, or vegetables, and a tagine of fish, served in the peaked stoneware for which the dish is named. Desserts include *bastilla*, crispy leaves of pastry topped with vanilla cream and toasted almonds. The traditional belly dancers that entertain throughout the meal are another delight of this exotic restaurant.

With the lively atmosphere of an authentic brasserie along the Rue de Seine, the celebrated Chefs de France restaurant features such favorites as Croque Monsieur, the classic toasted ham-and-cheese sandwich; beef short ribs braised in Cabernet on a bed of polenta; and a traditional onion soup topped with Gruyère cheese.

At the Rose and Crown Dining Room in the

United Kingdom, meat pies, bangers and mash (sausages with mashed potatoes), and prime rib are on the menu, and desserts are a royal treat—including trifle, a traditional mixture of fruit and custard cake; a sticky toffee pudding; and apple blackberry crumble, served with sherry custard. If it's authentic fish and chips you crave, you can find them next door at the Yorkshire County Fish Shop.

Nestled under the Hôtel du Canada in an appropriately sublevel environment is Le Cellier Steakhouse, Canada's premiere restaurant. Le Cellier features "Canadian steakhouse" fare such as herb-crusted prime rib, filet mignon glazed with maple barbecue sauce, and Cheddar Cheese soup. The ales and beers served reflect Canada's brewing history.

Illuminations: Reflections of Earth

IllumiNations' nightly spectacle is the grand finale each day at Epcot. Dancing flames, cascading fountains, and eye-popping fireworks synchronized to a dramatic musical score light the skies and decorate World Showcase Lagoon. IllumiNations begins with a cosmic event that leads to a ballet of fire and "chaos," signifying the origins of the planet. The mayhem then transforms into a sea of floating pyrotechnic stars, setting the stage for the appearance of the show's centerpiece, the dramatically spinning Earth Globe. Covered with video screens in the shape of the continents, the steel-ribbed Earth Globe projects vivid images that celebrate both human diversity and the unified spirit of humankind, in the first spherical video display ever created. The LED-created pictures depict primal seas and forests and the development of famous cultural landmarks, including the Himalayas, the Sphinx, Easter Island statues, and Mount Rushmore. Diverse visages of famous people from around the world are captured on the sphere. The performance concludes with the Earth Globe opening up like a lotus flower as a giant fire torch rises forty feet into the air from its heart, and color-rich confetti fireworks create reflections across the rippling waters.

Illuminations by the Numbers	
1	infrared guidance system that moves the Earth Globe
19	torches surrounding the Lagoon, representing the first nineteen centuries of the common era. The torch that rises out of the Earth Globe represents the current (21st) era.
28	diameter in feet of the Earth Globe
34	locations that set off fireworks shells
37	nozzles that shoot propane flames from the inferno barge
40	water nozzles per each of four fountain barges
40	locations of computers used to run the show
56	famous faces shown on the Earth Globe
67	computers used to run the show
100	height in feet of the flames spurting from the inferno barge
258	strobe lights that emanate from the Earth Globe
350	weight in tons of the island the Earth Globe spins upon
1,105	fireworks shells that are launched
2,800	(and more) fireworks shells that explode
4,000	gallons of water per minute each fountain barge pumps
150,000	notes in the musical score
150,000	weight in pounds of the inferno barge
180,000	light-emitting diodes used on the Earth Globe
350,000	weight in pounds of the Earth Globe